Copyright © 2004 by Nord-Süd Verlag AG, Gossau Zürich, Switzerland
First published in Switzerland under the title *Der Nikolaustaler*.
English translation copyright © 2004 by North-South Books Inc., New York
All rights reserved. No part of this book may be reproduced or utilized in any form or by any means,
electronic or mechanical, including photocopying, recording, or any information storage and
retrieval system, without permission in writing from the publisher.

First published in the United States, Great Britain, Canada, Australia, and New Zealand in 2004
by North-South Books, an imprint of Nord-Süd Verlag AG, Gossau Zürich, Switzerland.
Distributed in the United States by North-South Books Inc., New York.

Library of Congress Cataloging-in-Publication Data is available.
A CIP catalogue record for this book is available from The British Library.
ISBN 0-7358-1955-6 (trade edition)
1 3 5 7 9 HC 10 8 6 4 2
ISBN 0-7358-1956-4 (library edition)
1 3 5 7 9 LE 10 8 6 4 2
Printed in Belgium

For more information about our books, and the authors and artists
who create them, visit our web site: www.northsouth.com

SANTA'S LUCKY CHARM

By Udo Weigelt
Illustrated by Rolf Siegenthaler

Translated by Marianne Martens

North-South Books / New York / London

Late one night, when all was quiet in the forest, the animals were awakened by a loud "Ho, ho, ho!" A whip cracked in the sky. And tiny sleigh bells rang through the air.

"What is it? What is it? Who's making so much noise?" shouted Porcupine excitedly.

The other animals crept drowsily out of their dens and looked up at the sky.

"Well, well. Will you look at that sleigh!" said Rabbit, scratching his head. "How does he get it to fly like that?"

"Well . . . ," said Porcupine thoughtfully.

"It can only mean one thing," Raccoon interrupted. "Tomorrow must be Christmas!"

The animals gazed longingly at the sleigh as it disappeared in the distance.

Suddenly, something shiny tumbled through the air and landed in the high branches of a tree. Raccoon raced up the tree after it.

"It looks like a gold coin," declared Raccoon.
"Santa must have dropped it," said Rabbit.
The animals shouted after Santa, but he was too far away to hear them.

"What should we do with it?" Porcupine asked.

"What do you mean *we?*" asked Raccoon. "I'm the one who found it."

"Well, that may be, but I'm sure I spotted it first," said Fox.

"So what? I'm the one who saw where it fell," said Rabbit.

"Let's ask Owl," said Porcupine. "She can decide who gets to keep it."

Owl thought for a long time.

"Well, the way I see it," she said, "the gold piece really doesn't belong to any of you. It belongs to Santa. He lost it, and I don't think he was planning on giving it to any of you as a present."

"What do you think we should we do with it?" asked Rabbit.

"Talk to each other, and I'm sure you'll figure out just what to do," said Owl.

"It doesn't look as though Santa's coming back for his gold coin," said Porcupine. "How would he even know where to look for it?"

"Owl is right. Santa didn't give the coin to any of us," said Raccoon. "Animals don't have any use for gold coins. Only people do."

"Then we should give the coin to a person," said Rabbit. "You know, as a Christmas present!"

"Yes, let's!" Raccoon agreed. "It will be our turn to play Santa."

Everyone liked that idea.

"I know just the right person," said Fox. "We can give it to the old woodcutter who lives in the forest. He certainly seems very kind, and I think he's all alone except for his reindeer. I'm sure he'd be very happy to get it!"

That was the perfect solution. Owl *had* been right. The animals *did* know just what to do. Off they went to make their delivery.

When the animals arrived at the barn, everything was quiet and dark. The barn door was open, and the reindeer were gone.

"How odd," said the Rabbit. "Where did they go in the middle of the night?"

"It *is* strange," Porcupine agreed.

The animals were trying to figure out where to leave the gold coin when once again they heard the sound of sleigh bells.

Santa's sleigh landed right in front of them! The animals were shocked to see Santa, and Santa was even more shocked to see the animals.

"What brings you here?" he asked.

Shyly, Porcupine began, "We found your gold coin, and we didn't know how to get it back to you, so . . ."

"So we decided to use it to make the old woodcutter happy," continued Fox.

Santa laughed. "I see!" he said. "Usually it's *my* job to deliver the presents, but I think you have all done a very good thing. It was kind of you to think of this old wood-cutter. Why, it's the first time anyone's brought Santa himself a gift!"

"What?" exclaimed Rabbit. "*You're* the woodcutter?"

"Yes indeed!" Santa laughed. "And that coin that you found is my lucky charm! I always carry it with me. It must have fallen out of my pocket."

Santa unhitched the reindeer from his sleigh. Then he showed the animals his workshop, because of course they were all very curious.

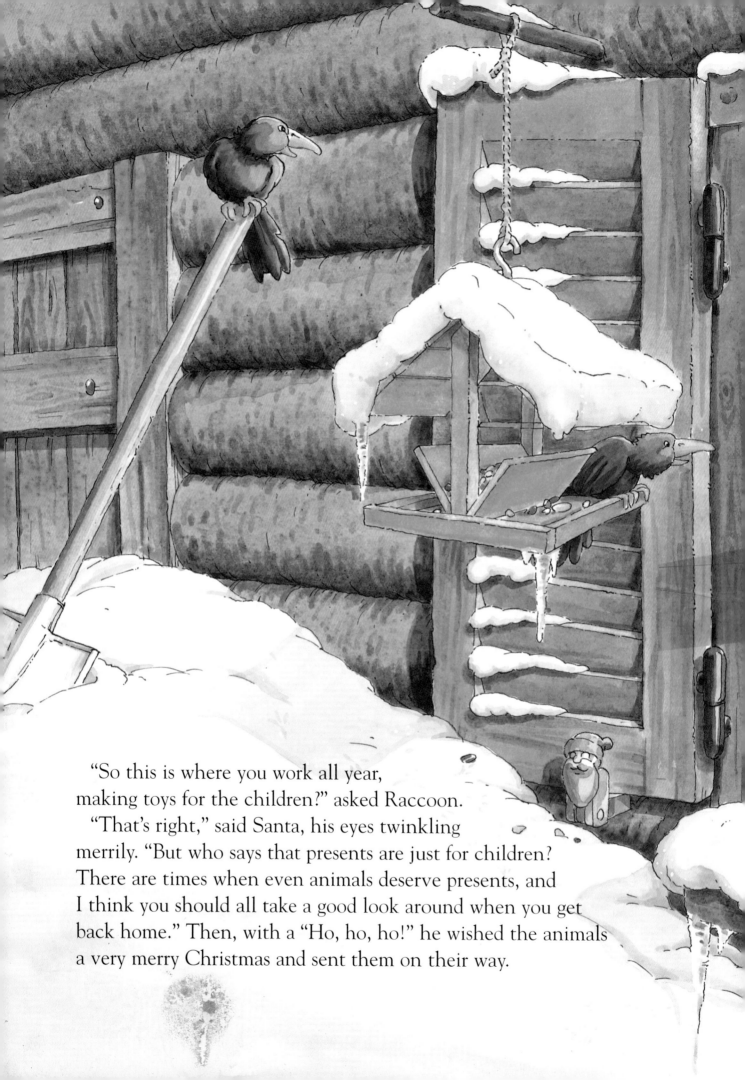

"So this is where you work all year,
making toys for the children?" asked Raccoon.

"That's right," said Santa, his eyes twinkling
merrily. "But who says that presents are just for children?
There are times when even animals deserve presents, and
I think you should all take a good look around when you get
back home." Then, with a "Ho, ho, ho!" he wished the animals
a very merry Christmas and sent them on their way.